This edition published exclusively
for Marks and Spencer p.l.c.
by Purnell Books, Paulton, Bristol BS18 5LQ,
a member of the BPCC group of companies
ISBN 0 361 06005 X
'Dangermouse' copyright © 1982
Cosgrove Hall Productions Limited

Text and illustrations copyright © 1983
Purnell Publishers Limited
Published August 1983
Made and printed in Great Britain
by Purnell and Sons
(Book Production) Limited, Paulton, Bristol

DANGER MOUSE

STRIKES AGAIN

Adapted by Greg Steddy
from the original television
scripts by Brian Trueman
Illustrated by
Michael Wells Studio

St Michael

Business was going on as usual at the headquarters of the International Egg Company in London. The Managing Director was dictating a letter to Baron von Greenback.

"For a chicken to be as tall as you suggest in your letter it would have had to have come from a giant egg. But, to acquire a giant egg you would need a giant chicken. To get a giant chicken you would need a giant . . ."

He was interrupted by a sudden scream from his secretary.

"A giant hen!" she exclaimed.

"No, no—*egg,*" he corrected.

"A hen, a giant hen!" she repeated in terror. "Out there!"

The Managing Director looked mildly surprised and followed the direction in which she was pointing. He started in panic as he came face to face with a most ferocious fowl.

"Aaaagh, a giant hen!" he screamed, running for the door as the hen burst through the window.

Meanwhile, in his secret Baker Street hideout, the world's greatest secret agent was having breakfast.

"This egg's a bit on the hard side, Penfold," said Dangermouse.

"Perhaps its mother was a bricklayer!" suggested Penfold.

Just then the videophone came on.

"Scramble, scramble, scramble," said the voice of Colonel K.

"It was boiled," said Penfold, puzzled.

"Trouble, sir?" asked Dangermouse.

"Big trouble, DM," replied Colonel K. "There's been a theft— new wonder drug. Makes things grow. Foreign chappie was showing it at a conference and poof—it was gone! Got a film of the chappie here. Professor Squvawkencluck."

A white-coated scientist appeared on the screen.

"Und here ve have ze chicken, very nice with schprouts and chips but too small! Mother, father, two cheeldren and a leetle pussycat. Munch, munch—all gone!

But I, von Squvawkencluck have zee answer. Bigger chickens! Chickens 500 foots tall! Then how many can munch? hundreds, thousands!

"And here is my seecret!" continued the Professor, taking a small test tube from his pocket. "My fantastiche super-duper serum . . ."

At that moment a dark shadowy figure passed across the screen, knocked down the Professor and seized the serum. The film ended and Colonel K reappeared.

"Mmm, I think I recognised that shadowy figure," said Dangermouse, thoughtfully. "It is none other than my old enemy Baron Greenback!"

"The unscrupulous villain!" roared Colonel K.

"Don't worry, sir," said Dangermouse. "We'll get it back—or my name isn't Dangermouse!"

"Er . . . isn't it?" asked Penfold, puzzled.

"Of course it is," retorted Dangermouse. "Come on!"

Dangermouse and Penfold were soon speeding through the city in Dangermouse's supercar. They stopped in the city centre and set off in opposite directions to search.

"I'm not sure I like this—sending me off on my own," muttered Penfold. "Hello, what's this?" He found himself staring at a huge pair of claws and slowly looked up . . .

"Good grief! A squvawkenclucking super-duper chicken! Aagh!"

He started to run, chased by the chicken who was gaining fast on poor Penfold. His legs wobbled with fear and he puffed and panted so much that his glasses steamed up and he couldn't see.

At last, exhausted, he slumped against a lamp post. The super-duper chicken squawked as it saw its prey almost within reach. Just as Penfold feared the worst Dangermouse arrived, dragged him into the car and headed off at high speed. As they made their escape Penfold cried: "Look out!"

A giant egg was falling through the sky. It landed on the car and broke open.

"Penfold, we've got a problem," said Dangermouse.

"What's that, sir?"

"Where can we get a rasher of bacon five yards long?"

"Very good, sir!" chuckled Penfold.

They were not out of danger yet. With the tireless chicken still in pursuit they drove at top speed, winding through back streets, climbing up mountains and weaving through woods all over England. Still the chicken followed them.

"What kind of a chicken is it, DM?" Penfold asked.

"Has it got two wires sticking out of its head?"

"No."

"Oh, well it's not a battery chicken then!"

Dangermouse was beginning to wonder how he could ever lose the chicken when suddenly he hit on a plan.

"Ow! That hurt!" he exclaimed.

"What hurt?" asked puzzled Penfold.

"I just hit on a plan," explained Dangermouse. "We'll really fool the fowl this time. Hold tight. We're putting out to sea."

As the amphibious car headed out to sea Penfold turned for a last look at the terrifying chicken.

"Crikey, sir, it's following us. Chickens can't swim."

"Tell it, Penfold, perhaps it doesn't know!"

"Oh, crikey," wailed Penfold. "We're going to be pecked to death by a pullet."

"No, Penfold, not a pullet," squeaked Dangermouse. "We're going to be plucked by a pigeon!" They had reached land again and were on a collision course with a huge pigeon. Dangermouse swerved and the car screeched to a halt.

"Looks like Greenback's got us penned in this time," said Dangermouse as the pigeon landed behind them.

"Oh, bad show, DM!" answered the pigeon. "Chap's a stinker!"

"Do you mean you're not one of Greenback's villains?" asked Dangermouse with relief.

"Abso-bally-lutely! Fella's a bounder. My name's Pigeon. Flying Officer Buggles Pigeon. One of Colonel K's chaps actually."

"Great," said Dangermouse. "Any news, Buggles?"

"Rather! I was zooming in with a message when I spotted the foul play. *Fowl* play, what! Ha ha!" laughed Buggles. "Seem's the beastly Baron has his HQ at a chicken farm in Kent."

"Then that's our target!" said Dangermouse. "Can you fly us there, Buggles? Let's get out of here before that chicken arrives."

Within minutes Buggles found the farm. He nose dived and crashed-landed in some trees.

"Oooops, sorry, chaps," he blustered as Dangermouse and Penfold picked themselves up.

"Come on, Penfold, head for the sheds!" commanded Dangermouse.

"It isn't half dark, sir!" whispered Penfold as they crept in.

"Don't worry, Penfold," said Dangermouse blithely.

"No, don't worry, Penfold," said a strange voice.

"Why are you using a funny voice, sir?" asked Penfold.

"I'm not using a funny voice."

At that moment they heard a loud clang, a light went on, and they found themselves in a cage facing the evil Baron Greenback.

"The terrible toad!" exclaimed Dangermouse.

Greenback turned to Nero, his pet caterpillar, often known as the powder puff.

"What shall we do with the nice gentlemen, my treasure?"

"Grrrrrrrrr, razzz, razz," replied Nero.

"What a nice idea . . ." purred Greenback.

'You won't get away with this, you green horror!" shouted Dangermouse sharply.

"Temper, temper," replied Greenback in a soothing voice. "Let me amuse you with my plan to rule the world!

"Dear old Squvawkencluck has given me the key. My little
chicks love his serum. They grow big and strong, but their eggs
look normal." Greenback cackled and then continued:

"I shall have these eggs delivered all over the world with the
morning milk. And when they hatch . . . hee hee hee!" Greenback
laughed convulsively. "I shall rule the world! But you won't be
around to see it! Stiletto, the lever!"

Greenback's evil henchman, Stiletto, pulled a lever and
Dangermouse and Penfold vanished through the floor. They found
themselves surrounded by giant chickens.

"Try not to look like a worm, Penfold," said Dangermouse, eyeing the chickens. "I'll hold them off while you dive for it."

"Right, sir," said Penfold, and dived straight into the giant chickens' water dish.

"Not that sort of dive!" wailed Dangermouse. "Good grief," he cried as Penfold suddenly emerged growing rapidly, "it's the Professor's growing serum!"

Penfold burst from the cage, a veritable giant towering over the chickens. He reached down and picked Dangermouse up.

"Penfold, you're a national hero!"

"Aw, thanks, sir. Mum always wondered what I'd be."

Penfold popped Dangermouse safely in his pocket and began rounding up the chickens.

"I expect the Professor will know what to do with them, chief," he said as he closed the cage.

"Don't let Greenback get away!" called a voice from his pocket.

But the Baron had once again given them the slip.

"Oh, crumbs," gasped Penfold. "That rather leaves us with egg on our faces!"

"Very funny!" muttered Dangermouse.

"Any hope?" asked the Colonel.

"Professor Squvawkencluck seems to think the stuff may wear off in the rain . . ." answered Dangermouse uncertainly.

"But it's not rainin'," objected Colonel K.

"It is on Penfold, sir," said Dangermouse.

Outside, towering over even the Post Office Tower, stood Penfold, looking very miserable as he held a watering can over his head. Catching sight of Dangermouse at the window he called out:

"What's for lunch, sir?"

"Chicken soup," answered Dangermouse.

Penfold shuddered and said: "I don't think I'm very hungry . . ."

THE INVASION OF COLONEL K

Deep in the heart of London, in an innocent-looking plumbers yard, Greenback was hatching another evil plan. This time he intended to infiltrate the very nerve centre of government intelligence—Colonel K himself!

He turned to Stiletto with a gleam in his eye (they are more effective than contact lenses!) and proclaimed grandly:

"I, the inventor of the Frog's Head Flyer—the most ingenious machine ever invented by any toad—am about to convert it into the most irresistible assault craft in the universe!"

"Oh," said Stiletto blankly. "How, Barone?"

"How?" echoed Greenback contemptuously. "With that ray!"

"Barone, I'm not Ray—I'm Stiletto!"

"Idiot!" snapped the Baron. "The Minimising Pica-Ray will shrink us, Flier and all, to microscopic size! Just press that button!"

As Stiletto pressed the button a strange ray enveloped the Flyer and it slowly shrank until it was no larger than a pin-head. When the shrinking had stopped the ship took off at high speed.

"Hey, Barone," stammered Stiletto. "Where-a we-a going?"

"To seize the secrets of the world!" exclaimed Greenback.

"Where from?" asked the puzzled Stiletto.

"From the brain cells of Colonel K! Ha, ha!" cackled the toad.

In his Mayfair hideout Dangermouse was at a loose end.

"You know, Penfold, if we don't get some action soon we'll start putting weight on."

"Mmm," agreed Penfold contentedly. "I always wanted to be a seventeen stone weakling."

At that moment the videoscreen crackled into life and Colonel K appeared.

"K to DM! K to DM!"

"Right, sir! We're ready, sir," answered Dangermouse eagerly. "Ready to save the universe from evil. So, the world is in peril, eh, sir? No matter, we are ready . . ."

"No, Dangermouse," interrupted the Colonel. "No. Matter of fact there's no business at all."

Dangermouse stared dumbly in disbelief.

"No danger, no evil, no work," confirmed the Colonel. "Thought we could all take a break. Have a week's leave—pair of you. I'm goin' to get some shut-eye." And with that the screen went blank.

"Good grief, Penfold, a week's leave!" repeated Dangermouse incredulously. "I think I'll put on a track suit and go for a run. What are you going to put on, Penfold?"

"Weight, DM," murmured Penfold smiling.

COLONEL 'K'

Meanwhile Greenback's microscopic Flyer was fast approaching Colonel K's office.

"Ha, ha, Stiletto, the target is in sight!" chuckled Greenback, as they glided through the keyhole, heading for Colonel K's ear.

"Huh? Wha'? What was that?" mumbled K, waking briefly as the Frog's Head Flyer buzzed into his ear.

"Quickly, Stiletto, to his hand!" commanded Greenback as they sped through K's insides. Greenback pressed the buttons marked 'fingers', making the Colonel switch on the videophone.

"Ah, er, Dangerfold. There you—er—are." stammered the confused Colonel.

"To his voice-box, Stiletto. Hurry!" whispered Greenback.

"Ah, Colonel!" exclaimed Dangermouse. "Is this the call to action that we have been waiting for?"

"Er . . . No, Dangermouse. Bad news, I'm afraid. You've been fired—and Penfold."

"Wha . . .? Why?" began Dangermouse in amazement.

"Government half-backs—er, cutbacks," waffled the Colonel.

"But, sir . . ." began Dangermouse.

"Silence, you wretched rodent! Your days are finished! And you'll have to leave the flat. Goodbye, forever!"

"Hee, hee, hee!" screeched Greenback, as he switched off. "Victory forever!" Now, to his brain, Stiletto! And then the secrets of the world will be mine!"

Dangermouse and Penfold were shocked and saddened by K's strange behaviour.

"I can't think what's got into him!" said Dangermouse as he packed his things. "Ah, well, goodbye old flat . . . We've had some happy times . . ."

"Oh, chief," wailed Penfold. "What'll we do?"

"We'll just find ourselves another job," replied Dangermouse, trying hard to be bright.

But jobs for secret agents don't grow on trees and the unfortunate pair soon found themselves sweeping the streets. The dreariness of the work was only broken by the sound of the radio as they swept their way from Willesden Green to Fulham.

One morning, as they were sweeping up the leaves in Kensington Gardens, Penfold suddenly stopped. A familiar voice on the radio caught his attention.

"Hey, chief, listen!" he shouted, turning up the volume. From the radio came the voice of Professor Squawkencluck.

"Calling Dangermouse! Squawkencluck to Dangermouse! If you are hearing this, at vonce to my laboratory come! If you are not hearing this, svitch on, you idiot! It's a national crisis!"

"Good grief!" exclaimed Dangermouse, dropping his broom. "It's the Professor! Come on, Penfold!"

Within minutes they were in the Professor's laboratory.

"What's the problem?" asked Dangermouse calmly.

"It's Colonel K," explained the Professor. "He's crazy! He's sacking everyone! I tried to examine him—and he just sacked me!"

"OK, Professor, leave it to us," said Dangermouse confidently, as he marched straight into Colonel K's office. Squawkencluck listened anxiously to the loud bangs coming from within. Then the door swung open and Dangermouse and Penfold appeared carrying the Colonel, bound hand and foot.

"That's about wrapped it up," said Dangermouse. "Where do you want him, Professor?"

"On zer X-ray table place him, please. I want his brain to examine." It only took a moment for the Professor to discover that all was not well.

"Ha-ha! I thought he something on his mind had! Here, a foreign object. I will a close-up look take—Oh!" he gasped as the object came into focus. "Ze Frog's Head Flyer! Ze Baron has found a way to shrink it!"

"Good grief!" exclaimed Dangermouse. "Someone's got to go in after him! We have to find the Baron's shrinking device. Any ideas, Professor?"

"No doubt zis shrinking device will radiation give off. Take my Geiger counter and you'll soon track it down. I will with you come then I can operate ze device."

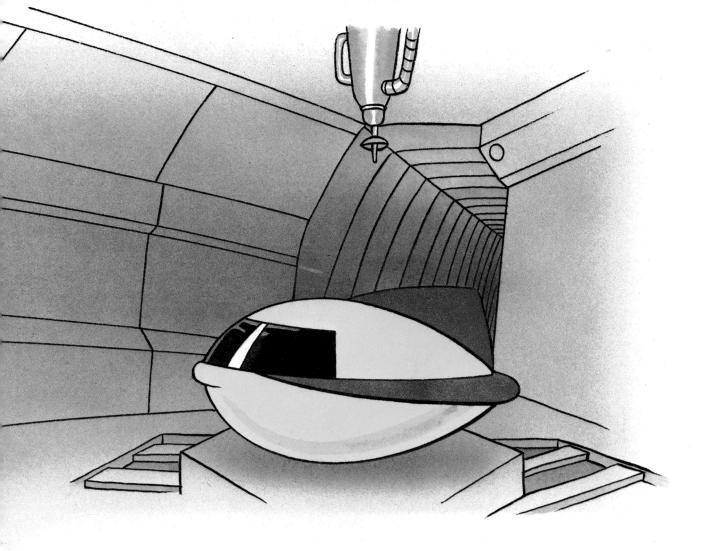

Soon Dangermouse, Penfold, Professor Squawkencluck and the bound Colonel K were all aboard the space hopper. Using the Professor's Geiger counter they tracked down the Baron's shrinking machine in his secret laboratory. It didn't take the Professor long to work out how to operate it.

"OK, ve place ze Colonel on ze table, so. Now you in ze space hopper with Penfold go, Dangermouse. Ready? Then I shrink you."

"Ooh, it tickles!" chuckled Penfold, as the ship swiftly shrank. Dangermouse steered the space hopper carefully along a dark passage inside the Colonel's head. He drew to a halt as they reached a fork.

"Which way do we go from here, Professor," asked Dangermouse over the radio.

"You just follow ze signs."

"Signs?" said Dangermouse scornfully. A sign saying Brain Department appeared. "Good grief, he's right, Penfold!"

"Hee, hee, hee!" cackled Greenback, who was watching the hopper on his video monitor. "The fools! Little do they know that I switched the signs. They're on their way to his feet! Now to jam the radio!"

"Crumbs, chief," exclaimed Penfold, as they sped through an artery. "What are those?"

Small, round creatures, carrying buckets were everywhere.

"Those are red blood corpuscles. They're taking carbon dioxide to the lungs and . . ."

"Look out, chief!" screamed Penfold, as they bumped into a corpuscle. A whole cluster of them quickly surrounded the ship.

"Oo, crumbs. I think we've been mistaken for a germ," groaned Penfold, as the corpuscles hurled buckets of carbon dioxide at them.

"Hold tight, Penfold. If I turn sharply down here I think I can throw them off."

They found themselves in a very dark place. Penfold was fumbling for the light switch when suddenly there was a loud roar.

"Aaaagh! Help!" he screamed.

The creature that had roared burst into fits of laughter.

"Oo-ha, ha,ha! That had yer! Funny Bone's the name and laughter's the game. 'Ere—'ave a custard pie!"

"That, my friend, is *not* funny," said Dangermouse crossly, as he wiped custard from his face.

"He wants dislocating!" grumbled Penfold. They made a hasty exit and turned back into a main artery.

"Thank goodness, Penfold. We're on the right path at last," said Dangermouse as they entered a spacious area.

"Cor, chief, there's a terrible draught in here," moaned Penfold.

"Good grief, germs hang-gliding," gasped Dangermouse. "Wait a minute! There's only one place where there's room for that. We must be in the lungs!"

"But the signs said to the brain," objected Penfold.

"Curse it! Greenback's changed the signs. That means . . ."

"We're lost!" cried Penfold. "Help! Help! We're lost!"

"Steady on, Penfold. We just go back the way we came."

They shot off at high speed but came to a halt as an army checkpoint loomed ahead.

"Halt!" bawled a Sergeant Major. "Where is your passport?"

"My . . .?" Dangermouse stammered in amazement.

"Passport! You 'eard, lad! We are lookin' for two intruders in a space hopper."

"Excuse me, er, Sergeant Major, sir!" called another soldier.

"Yes, what is it, lad?" asked the Sergeant Major.

Whilst he was distracted Dangermouse put his foot down and they sped forward, heedless of the angry cries behind.

"Crumbs, chief! More of them," called Penfold, as they approached a platoon of soldiers. Dangermouse made a quick turn down a side tunnel—but it was blocked by another of the Colonel's body defences, an excavator which was making straight for them.

"Oo, chief, whatever shall we do?" squealed Penfold.

Meanwhile, untroubled by Dangermouse, Greenback had reached his goal—the vaults of Colonel K's memory banks.

"Right, Stiletto, let's take a look at these secrets. Quick, play one through!" commanded Greenback excitedly.

Stiletto took a video from the rack and fed it into the Frog's Head Flyer's computer. Colonel K appeared on the screen.

"Ah, Miss Hackett. With milk and two lumps . . . Great Scott! What's goin' on?"

"Poor fool," taunted Greenback. "*I* am going on—to rule the world with *your* memory."

"What! You bounder!" exclaimed K, reaching for a button. As he pressed it alarm bells began ringing.

"Whoa! What's going on?" wailed Penfold, as they were suddenly thrown sideways. The alarm system had made the Colonel sit up with a jolt, throwing Dangermouse and Penfold off balance.

"The Baron must have made it to K's brain," explained Dangermouse. "My guess is that the Colonel's alerting his body's defences."

"Yes, you're right! Look!" cried Penfold, as soldiers rushed past. "They're going to fight the Baron!"

Dangermouse and Penfold hurried after them. As they approached K's brain a videoscreen crackled into life and they drew to a halt.

"Reg'men'al Sarn't Major reportin' for duty, sir!" barked the Sergeant Major to the image of K on the screen.

"Good!" said K. "Seek out invaders!"

With that the whole platoon turned on Dangermouse and

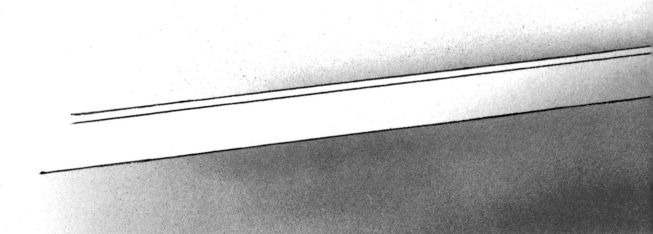

Penfold and began to attack them. They were only prevented by
Colonel K who was shouting "No, no. That mouse is on our side!"

"No, sah!" replied the Sergeant Major. " 'E is an outsider, sah!"

"Don't argue with me, Sergeant Major," bawled K. "Listen,
DM. It's Greenback. He's grabbed me memories and shot off for
me ear! Get after him . . ."

Dangermouse was already on his way with the soldiers.

"It's no good," he panted, stopping for a moment. "We can't
head them off. There's only one way . . . All together – shout!"
There was a deafening chorus of *'Greenback'* which set up

reverberations in Colonel K's eardrum. The villains were bounced from side to side and dropped all the tapes they were carrying. They finally bounced straight out of K's ear.

"You've done it, DM!" exclaimed Penfold.

"Yes, I thought I might," said Dangermouse coolly. "Sergeant Major, put all those tapes back and get rid of the two space ships. Penfold, we've got to move! I think the shrink ray's wearing off."

They leapt from the Colonel's right ear, growing rapidly.

"Well, Squawkencluck, we did it!" exclaimed Dangermouse. "But I'm afraid Greenback got away."

"A job well done!" congratulated the Professor.

"Well, it was certainly memorable!" said Dangermouse. "Now I know what it feels like to be at the *head* of the Secret Service!"

"**H**ey, Penfold, why is my rubber duck full of water?" called Dangermouse from the bathroom. "Have you been using it as a water pistol again? Penfold? *Pen—fold!*"

"Yes, DM, what is it?" answered Penfold hurriedly.

"Do you know my rubber duck's full of water?"

"No, chief, but if you hum it, I'll join in on the second chorus!"

"Good grief!" muttered Dangermouse to himself. "He must do it on purpose—no-one could be *that* silly!"

At that moment the doorbell rang and Penfold ran to answer it.

"The Dangermouse residence," he said formally into the intercom. "His faithful assistant, Penfold, here—can I help you?"

"No, short stuff!" replied an evil voice. "It's your boss I want!"

"Well," continued Penfold. "I'm afraid he's busy conducting some experiments into the amphibious hydrodynamics of modular elasticity!"

"Don't give me that!" snapped the voice. "When he's finished playing with his rubber duck, just tell him that the Demon of the Fourth Dimension invites him to save the world from the chaos into which I shall plunge it!"

"C-c-crikey, chief!" cried Penfold in alarm. "Th-there's a demon duck from the rubber dimension, and er, he's g-going to . . ."

"That's all right, Penfold," interrupted Dangermouse calmly. "I heard. We'd better put a stop to his foul deeds. Come on!"

They raced off in the car but within seconds screeched to a halt.

"Hey, chief," said Penfold with a puzzled frown. "We're stopping. But we'll lose it!"

"Lose what?" asked Dangermouse. "We don't know what it looks like!"

"I do, chief!" babbled Penfold. "It's got great big bulging eyes, and teeth, and . . ."

"And I think we'd better contact Colonel K," cut in Dangermouse. "The world will have to be alerted!"

Before he could make a move, the Demon's disembodied eyes appeared above them.

"Crikey, sir!" wailed Penfold. "What did I tell you?"

"Steady, Penfold!" said Dangermouse boldly. "I've locked the car doors so there's no way he can . . ."

His words tailed off as the car suddenly exploded around them.

"You fiend!" cried Dangermouse angrily. "What have you done with my car?"

"I've parked it for you!" screeched the Demon. "In the Fourth Dimension!"

"You expect me to believe *that?*" scoffed Dangermouse.

"Watch this then, unbeliever!" chortled the Demon, as Dangermouse's head suddenly disappeared.

"Oh crikey!" cried Penfold in alarm. "He's gone all to pieces and lost his head!"

"Don't panic, Penfold," called Dangermouse. "I'm just over here in the Fourth Dimension—well, my head is!"

"Hee hee!" giggled the Demon. "I am the master of time and space. I can make myself bigger or smaller. I alone can forge the inter-cosmic fragments into a whole!"

"A hole, eh?" muttered Dangermouse. "Just what I need!" He leapt up and pulled his body into the Fourth Dimension.

"There!" he cried triumphantly. "Now, it's about time I forged *you* into inter-cosmic fragments!"

Dangermouse made a dive for the demon, but to his surprise found himself grasping at thin air.

"Ha!" jeered the Demon. "You'll have to be quicker than that!"

He sent Dangermouse plunging back into the third dimension.

"Cor, chief, you're back!" cried Penfold with relief. "Now what we need is a way out!"

"And what you're going to get . . ." sniggered the Demon, materialising above them, ". . . is a blackout!"

Everything went completely dark, and they found themselves in a tunnel, stumbling blindly forwards.

"Oh, crumbs, chief!" quavered Penfold. "Where are we? We're lost, aren't we? I know it!"

"Penfold!" said Dangermouse sternly. "Pull yourself together. We'll find a way out. My sense of direction is perfect." With that Dangermouse set off along the tunnel with Penfold very close behind. After a while he paused, looked around and said: "You know, Penfold, I think we may have taken a wrong turning . . ."

After many miles and several hours of wandering the weary pair finally surfaced near Tower Bridge.

"I say, sir," said Penfold, cautiously. "I could have sworn this was where the Tower should be – but it seems to have disappeared."

"There can be only one explanation," answered Dangermouse. "The Demon has stolen it."

In fact the Demon had been hard at work whilst they were underground. He had stolen famous buildings from all over the world and transported them back to the Fourth Dimension.

"But how?" asked puzzled Penfold.

"All the Demon has done is make a time corridor between our

dimension and his—and slipped the Tower through it!"

"Oh, is that all?" said Penfold blankly.

"So all *we* have to do is slip through after him!" continued Dangermouse. "He's left a door that we can use."

"I can't see one," said Penfold, looking around.

'Of course not," retorted Dangermouse. "It's invisible."

"Oh, well, if you'd said that in the first place I'd have known what to look for—I think," said Penfold in utter confusion.

"Come on, Penfold. There's no time to lose," urged Dangermouse.

They stepped through the door and found themselves wandering in a weird landscape. Suddenly the Demon appeared, towering awesomely above them.

"Crikey, chief!" wailed Penfold. "He was never that big before! I don't like to be a nuisance but, I think I'm going to panic!"

"No time for that!" said Dangermouse grimly. "Run for it!"

They raced backwards and forwards through a maze of tunnels and passages until they were quite lost.

"Quickly, chief!" cried Penfold in alarm. "I can hear footsteps!"

"They're *mine,* Penfold!" said Dangermouse wearily.

Suddenly they both disappeared through a trapdoor.

"Crikey, chief," wailed Penfold. "What are we going to do?"

"Would you believe—faaaall!!"

With a large splash, they landed in a Fourth Dimensional sea. A mysterious submarine surfaced silently behind them and blasted them with cannons.

"Another of the Demon's tricks!" muttered a blackened Dangermouse. "And this looks like another!"

A pack of hungry sharks swam menacingly around them.

"There's only one thing to do," cried Dangermouse. "It's worked before, so it might work now!"

"What's that, chief?" asked Penfold desperately.

"Well, we'll simply—PANIC!!"

They leapt out of the water and fled along the shore, but still the Demon tormented them with tricks and trapdoors and tripwires. Finally, Dangermouse could stand it no longer.

"Now look here, sunshine!" he cried, addressing the Demon. "I hope you're a fully paid-up member of the 4-D Union!"

"Course I am!" boasted the Demon. "So what?"

"Can I remind you of Rule 4, brackets (b), para. 57, section A, sub-section 3c," continued Dangermouse, "which clearly states that any victims not destroyed by this stage of the proceedings have to be returned to their own dimension, or your powers are revoked by the Chief Demon!"

"All right, all right," agreed the Demon hastily. "You can go back to your own dimension, but please don't tell on me!"

"Cor, chief, you're a genius!" said Penfold in admiration. "We're back! Lucky you knew those Union rules!"

"No, Penfold," said Dangermouse. "It's lucky *he* didn't! There's no such rule—I fooled him!"

"Er, well, that's fair enough," gulped Penfold anxiously, "cos he's fooled us! Look!"

Dangermouse looked, and saw that the Demon had returned them to their dimension—but had left them suspended about four hundred feet above the ground. Without even time to call out he found himself plummetting through the air. They both landed with a crash in the middle of Trafalgar Square.

"I've had enough of this," groaned Dangermouse. "Let's have a spot of lunch at the club!"

"But the Demon!" cried Penfold. "Won't he follow us?"

"If he does, he won't get in without a tie!"

"But *you* do, chief!"

"That's because I'm a national hero and . . ."

His words were interrupted by an angry roar from the Demon who suddenly appeared before them, larger and fiercer than ever.

"Just in time for a demonstration of my awesome powers!" he boomed. "I'm going to eat the entire city of London for lunch—

and guess who's going to be the cherry on the top?"

"Well, that's it then," said Dangermouse meekly. "You're too good for me. I wonder if I might have a last request?"

"Poor little pipsqueak!" sneered the Demon. "All right—what do you want?"

"Well," continued Dangermouse. "Young Penfold here's not too bright, and I don't think he understands quite how powerful you are. It would be a shame if we popped off without him realising how brilliantly you won the contest."

"Right then," said the Demon, clearly flattered. "You explain it and I shall give you a demonstration."

"Well, now," began Dangermouse, describing the Demon's powers to Penfold. "This genius can create a time corridor, connecting a door in our own dimension to one in his own."

"Clever!" gasped Penfold.

"Wait!" said the Demon. "I open this door . . ." And he stepped through a door that had appeared from nowhere. "Then I open this door—into the Fourth Dimension . . ." he called.

"Now," said Dangermouse. "All we have to do is close *that* door . . ." He slipped along the time corridor after the Demon and slammed the door into the Fourth Dimension.

"Then we close *this* door . . ." he continued, as he raced back past the Demon and slipped back into his own dimension. He slammed the door behind him and gave a cry of triumph.

"Now he's not in his dimension or in ours. He's powerless!"

"He's trapped! Whoopee!" yelled Penfold, leaping up and down.

"Unless some idiot opens the door!" warned Dangermouse. "So, keep your hands in your pockets—I've got to make a phone call."

"... So how did you get rid of this blasted Demon, DM?" asked
Colonel K, as Dangermouse reported the whole story.

"Well, Colonel," chuckled Dangermouse. "I called up a friend of
mine at NASA who's in the removal business!"

"The *removal* business, DM?" asked the Colonel in amazement.

"That's right, Colonel," laughed Dangermouse. "He removed
the door *and* the Demon—to Alpha Centauri!"

THE ODD BALL RUN·A·ROUND

Way down under, in the middle of the Australian outback, Dangermouse and Penfold had just completed another successful mission.

"Right, Penfold, back to base," said Dangermouse, heading for the car. "Penfold! Get rid of that boomerang . . ."

He was interrupted by a bleep from the car's videoscreen.

"That'll be Colonel K. Come on, Penfold."

"Ah, DM!" said K. "Our man in Sydney is holding some top secret plans, and his cover has been blown. The underworld's after him and he needs your help! You'll find him here." And with that Colonel K vanished and a map reference appeared on the screen.

"Right away, sir!" breathed Dangermouse. "I'll get those plans to you in London! I'm on my way! Penfold! *Penfold!* Get rid of that boomerang!"

Penfold reluctantly hurled the boomerang into the outback and joined Dangermouse in the car. They drove off at high speed, following the map reference which led them to a football pitch.

"Seems a funny place to meet an agent," mused Dangermouse.

"Still—it would be difficult for anything to sneak up on us," said Penfold as they stood in the centre of the pitch. Just then he was flattened by the boomerang, which had travelled behind the car for miles trying to return itself to Penfold in true Aussie fashion.

"I thought I told you to get rid of that thing," snapped Dangermouse irritably.

Penfold hurled it away once more.

"Here comes our man now!" cried Dangermouse as a large rat came racing towards them. "I bet someone's on his tail!"

The rat thrust a rugby ball at Dangermouse.

"DM! Plans in the ball! Hurry—they're after me!" he gasped, and ran on.

"Who are?" asked Dangermouse.

The rat hesitated.

"It's—ooof!" he cried, and fell down stunned as Penfold's boomerang returned and knocked him out cold.

"I don't recall a villain by the name of Ooof, do you, Penfold?" mused Dangermouse.

There was no time for Penfold to reply. A pack of nasty-looking scoundrels were heading towards them. Just in time, Dangermouse hailed a passing kangaroo with the truly British cry of 'Taxi!'—a call which never fails in a tight spot. Together the intrepid pair dived into its pouch and were transported back to the car.

"Keep the change," said Dangermouse, paying up as they hopped out.

"Good on yer, sport!" grinned the kangaroo, hopping away.

Dangermouse set off at high speed and didn't look back until they were deep in the outback. He parked the car and looked carefully around.

"I think we've lost them, Penfold," he declared. "But I'll just take a stroll to make sure the coast is clear. You stay here and look after the ball."

"Right, chief," said Penfold, settling down for a little snooze.

Dangermouse had just turned back when he was startled by a screech from Penfold. He ran back as fast as he could—just in time to see a huge, fierce bird whisking Penfold into the sky.

"Ow-ow!" cried Penfold. "Help!" He closed his eyes and clutched the ball tightly.

Not wasting a second, Dangermouse leapt into the car. But the bird flew fast and even in the Mark II he could hardly keep up.

At last it reached its nest, on a high ledge in the Swiss Alps. A hungry fledgling squawked eagerly as it saw breakfast arriving. Penfold scrambled hastily over the side of the nest, away from the snapping beak—and plummeted down the mountainside.

Dangermouse had lost the trail and stopped the car in the valley to look around, hoping to spot Penfold and the bird. As he started to drive on again Penfold bounced into the passenger seat.

"Ah, there you are. Where's the ball?" asked Dangermouse. Penfold shuddered.

"Oo chief! It was awful! We were flying over—er—that castle over there and I . . . I dropped it!"

"Butterfingers!" yelled Dangermouse. "We'll have to go and get it then, won't we!"

"Er—yes, DM! Sorry, DM!" twittered Penfold.

"Anyone at home?" called Dangermouse in a friendly way, as he stood some time later at the drawbridge to the moated castle. "Can we have our ball back, please?"

A large round object came hurtling through the air towards him. Dangermouse caught it.

"Thank you very much!" he called, catching it.

"Look out, DM!" screamed Penfold. "It's a bomb!"

There was a loud bang and Dangermouse vanished in a cloud of smoke. When the smoke cleared he was lolling nonchalantly against the rear of the car.

"Cor, chief!" said Penfold. "I thought you'd been . . ."

"Blown up?" smiled Dangermouse. "When I need to, Penfold, I can run fast."

"Are we going home?" asked Penfold eagerly.

"Hardly, Penfold. The plans are still in the castle, remember? Set up the box of gadgets!"

Penfold struggled with the huge box, while in the castle above a familiar pair of villains watched the proceedings.

"Eh, Barone! De bomb didn't put them off!" said Stiletto. "I thinka dey come after de ball!"

"Hmm. So it seems, Stiletto," said Greenback. "I will take it to the laboratory downstairs to see if my scientists can open it."

Outside Dangermouse stood bravely on the Secret Service Mark II rocket launcher.

"Right, Penfold," he said. "I'm ready. Fire!"

There was a huge bang and when the smoke cleared a rather burnt Dangermouse was still in position on the launch pad.

"Sorry," said Penfold, going red. "I forgot to remove the safety catch!"

The second attempt was more successful—if more painful. Dangermouse was blasted through the air only to be splattered against the wall of the castle, right beside the window where Stiletto smirked.

"Ugh! Don't go away—I'll be back!" promised Dangermouse as he slid down the wall into the moat below.

"In a wheelchair?" sneered Stiletto.

For the next attempt, Dangermouse sat astride a rocket. The only trouble was, it exploded as it embedded itself in the wall beside the window.

"Sorry about that, chief," quavered Penfold. "Nothing will go wrong this time . . ."

This time the rocket went straight in through the open window. It sped right across the room—and out through a window on the far side. Once again Dangermouse landed in the moat.

But Dangermouse was not the world's top secret agent for nothing. He climbed back up to the window with the aid of suckers on his hands and feet.

"All right in there, your time's up!" he snarled.

"But Signor Dangermouse, is only five-a to three!" whined Stiletto.

"Absolute nonsense!" said Dangermouse. "It's—er—" He took his hand from the wall to check the time by his wristwatch. Unfortunately the sucker was so powerful that it wrenched part of the wall away with it. Dangermouse plunged into the moat once more, weighed down by stones still firmly fixed to the sucker.

"Drop in any time!" crowed Stiletto.

A few minutes later Stiletto gasped in surprise.

"That's one crazy mouse! He's-a comin' to de front-a door!"

Unfortunately for Dangermouse, Greenback did not think it funny and he lowered the drawbridge on to Dangermouse's head.

Penfold wailed.

"I'm here, Penfold," chuckled Dangermouse, appearing behind him out of a tunnel he had drilled at top speed as the drawbridge fell. "Argh! Look!"

There was scarcely time for Penfold to turn and realise that Greenback had unleashed Mad Manuel, the flamenco assassin, before the fiend was upon them. A fight ensued.

But Dangermouse had, of course, been on a government training course in flamenco dancing and made short work of Manuel. Then he raced across the drawbridge into the castle.

"It's very dark in here," he thought.

Dangermouse had, in fact, run straight into the mouth of a cannon. A moment later he shot up through the roof and away beyond the horizon.

"Dangermouse has departed as planned," chuckled Stiletto to Greenback. "What shall I do with de little fellow?"

"Give him a room with a view," sneered Greenback.

Penfold found himself bound and gagged at the top of a flagpole.

The cannon had sent Dangermouse right up into the Alps, but he was undeterred and headed straight back to the castle on skis. Little did he guess the fiendish fate that Greenback had in store— —a pack of dreaded mouse-eating bananas!

The drawbridge was down. Dangermouse swept in on his skis. There were cries and shouts of "aagh!", "Ooof!" and the like. Then Dangermouse swept out with Penfold, clutching the ball.

"That's what I call a rescue, Dangermouse!" breathed Penfold, admiringly. "And it was great how you got those mouse-eating bananas to acquire a taste for frog!"

"I don't think the Baron would agree with you, Penfold!" chuckled Dangermouse.

Inside the castle, Nero watched calmly as his master was savaged by the bananas.

"Ah! Stop, you brutes! Fruits! I am your master! No! No-o-o!"
Dangermouse and Penfold flew along on the skis, finally
dropping gracefully down somewhere over the English Channel.
Luckily a ship happened to be passing underneath at that moment,
and even more luckily for our heroes it was going to England and
not in the opposite direction. So Dangermouse and Penfold got a
lift home—although Penfold was not too happy at landing in the
sooty funnel of the ship when there was plenty of deck nearby.

"Chin up, Penfold!" urged Dangermouse. "We did stop the top
secret plans from falling into Greenback's evil clutches!"

That evening, they reported to Colonel K on the videophone.

"You'll be pleased to learn, sir, that we got the top secret plans
back, safe and sound," said Dangermouse proudly.

"Oh! Jolly good show, Dangermouse," said Colonel K. "I say,
did you have any trouble?"

"None to speak of, sir."

Behind him, Penfold choked when he heard this. Dangermouse turned to him.

"Penfold, shush! The Colonel doesn't want to hear about our little problems. He's got more important things on his mind."

"Yes—like your next mission," said the Colonel.

"Our *next* mission?" said Dangermouse in surprise.

"Yes," said Colonel K. "I want you to get some dummy plans into Greenback's hands."

"Why, sir?"

Well, by the time he discovers they're false, I'll have put the real ones into operation. Dashed cunning plan, eh?"

"And where are these dummy plans?" asked Dangermouse.

"Eh? Oh—in that rugby ball!" replied the Colonel. "I say, Dangermouse, is anything the matter? Dangermouse?"

But Dangermouse couldn't answer for a moment. He was too busy consoling poor Penfold, who had collapsed in a sobbing, gibbering heap on his shoulder!